M
O
B
I
L
E
S

B
Y

FLENSTED

Mobiles are a traditional craft in Denmark, but the modern mobile was first created in 1954 by Christian Flensted and his wife, Grethe. Their original design, the Lucky Stork, was a great success and now flies all over the world. Today, their son Ole and his wife, Aase, continue the tradition, conceiving new and innovative designs in their "Department of Space Research." Each mobile—designed so that individual elements are in constant motion while the entire mobile maintains a harmonic balance—is assembled by hand. All of the Flensted mobiles can be seen on their web site at www.flensted-mobiles.com.

Counting is as easy as . . .

1

2

3

Count the chickens and count their eggs.

How
many
eggs
does
the
blue hen
have?

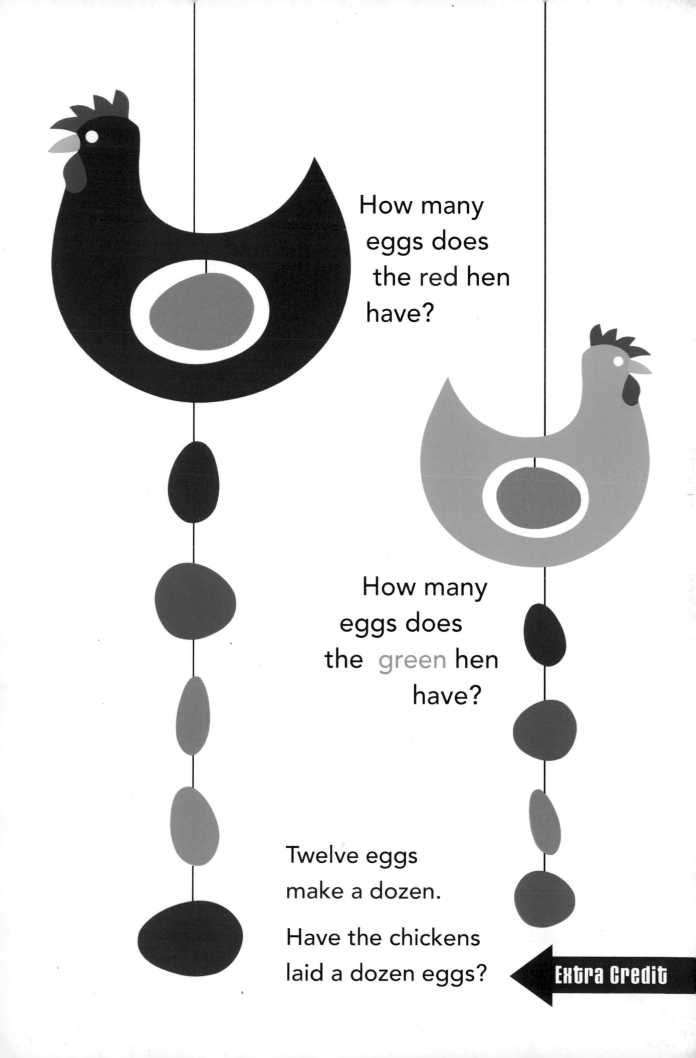

How many
eggs does
the red hen
have?

How many
eggs does
the green hen
have?

Twelve eggs
make a dozen.

Have the chickens
laid a dozen eggs?

Extra Credit

How many fish?

How
many
little
fish   did the
big fish
eat?

How
many
fish got
away?

Extra Credit

How many elephants?

How
many
blue
elephants?

How
many
yellow
elephants?

How many elephants in all?

Extra Credit

Three by
three ...
let's
count.

How
many
boats?

Toucans two by two...
count by twos.

How
many
red birds?

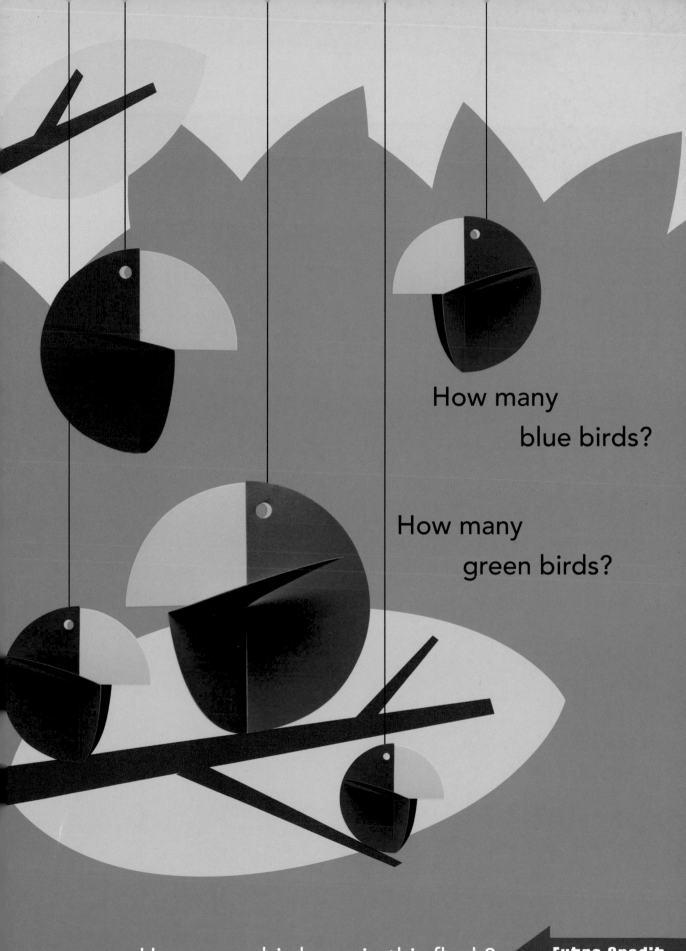

How many
blue birds?

How many
green birds?

How many birds are in this flock? Extra Credit
Count by twos.

How
many
bats?

How many cats and bats altogether?

Extra Credit

How many ways can you get to five?

$$1 + 4$$

$$2 + 3$$

$$3 + 2$$

Extra Credit How many hens and chicks altogether?

How many
on the ground and up in the air?

How many white sheep are on the grass?

How many ways can you get to six?

$$1 + 5$$

$$2 + 4$$

$$3 + 3$$

Extra Credit ➤ How many cats and balls altogether?

How many flying?

How many standing?

How many more penguins than geese?

How many birds in all?

Extra Credit

$$2 + 5$$
$$5 + 2$$

How many other ways can you get to seven?

How many in all?

Extra Credit

How many?

How
many
balls?

Extra Credit If a seal drops one of the balls, how many will be left?

If a clown drops two of the balls, how many will be left?

Extra Credit

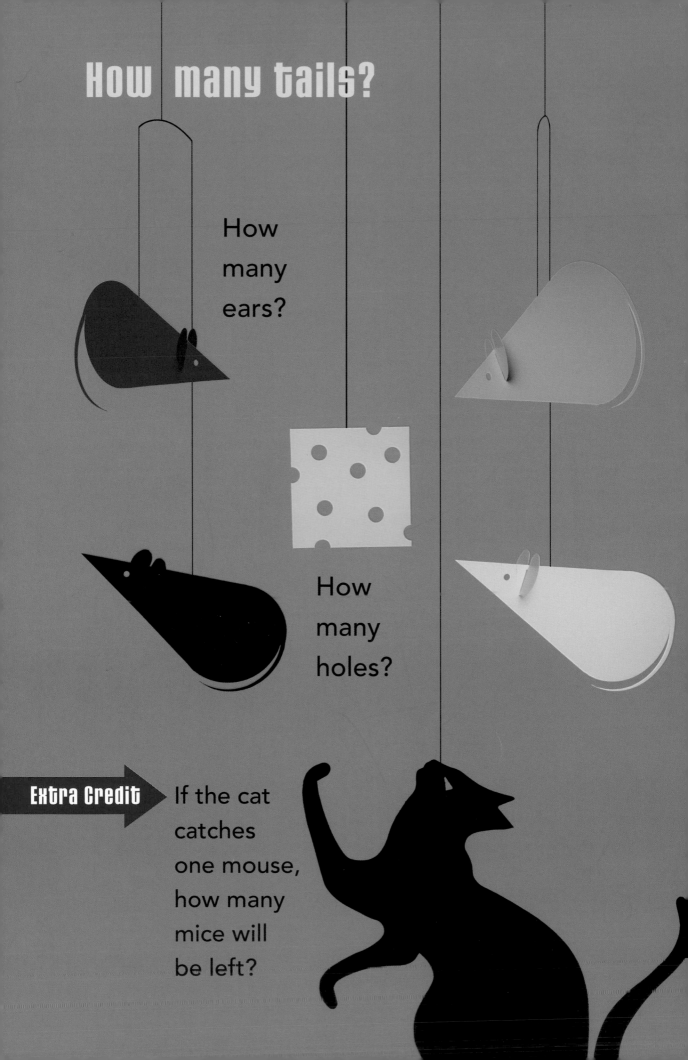

How many tails?

How
many
ears?

How
many
holes?

Extra Credit → If the cat
catches
one mouse,
how many
mice will
be left?

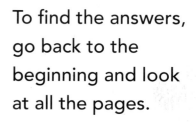

To find the answers,
go back to the
beginning and look
at all the pages.

EXTRA Extra Credit

How
many birds
are in
the
sky?

How
many
animals are
in the
water?

How many balls?